But each morning the king unlocked the door to find the princesses' shoes completely worn out.

It was as if they had been dancing all night.

So the king set a challenge. If a young man could discover where the princesses went at night, he could choose one to be his wife.

The Twelve Dancing Princesses

Miles

There was once a king who had twelve daughters. They slept in twelve beds in one big room.

When the princesses went to bed each night, the king locked their door.

Many accepted the challenge. They were given a room next to the princesses' chamber.

But every young man failed to stay awake. Each morning there was yet another pile of worn-out shoes.

A soldier passing by heard about the king's challenge. "I would like to marry a princess," he said.

Suddenly an old woman appeared.

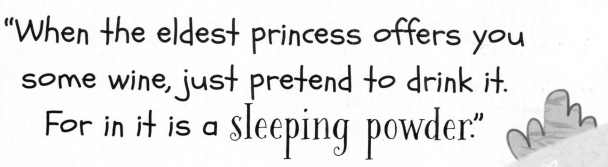

"When the eldest princess offers you some wine, just pretend to drink it. For in it is a sleeping powder."

The woman gave the soldier a magic cloak. "This will make you invisible, so you can follow the princesses."

At the castle, the soldier was shown to his room.

When the eldest princess gave him some wine, he tipped it away. Then he lay down and pretended to fall asleep.

The princesses dressed in dancing gowns and shoes. Then they opened a secret trapdoor and crept down the stairs.

The soldier put on the magic cloak and became invisible. He unlocked the door and followed the youngest princess down the stairs.

They came to a wood of golden trees. The soldier broke off a branch to take back to the king.

"Someone is following us!" said the youngest princess, but her sisters just laughed at her.

Then they came to a lake, upon which were twelve boats. In each boat was a handsome prince, waiting for a princess.

The soldier slipped onto the same boat as the youngest princess.

The princes rowed across the
lake to a shining castle. Then
they all went into the castle,
followed by the soldier.

Inside, the sound of trumpets, horns and drums could be heard. The princesses began to dance with their princes.

The invisible soldier tried to dance too.

The princesses became thirsty, but whenever they lifted a glass to drink, the soldier drank the glass dry.

The youngest princess was very frightened.

The princesses danced and danced, and did not stop until 3 o'clock in the morning, when their shoes were quite worn out.

They rowed back across the lake.
This time the soldier sat in the boat
with the eldest princess.

When the princesses arrived back in their chamber, they kicked off their worn-out shoes and fell fast asleep.

That morning, the king called for the soldier to have breakfast with him.

"Have you discovered where my daughters go and what they do?"

"Yes," said the soldier, and he showed the king the gold branch he had hidden under his magic cloak. He told the king exactly what he had seen.

"Wake the princesses!" the king cried.

Soon twelve sleepy princesses were stood in front of their father.

When they saw the gold branch, they had no choice but to tell the truth.

"Which princess would you
like to marry?" asked the king.
"The eldest princess," said the soldier.
They were married that day.

The princess taught the soldier how to dance, and they lived happily ever after.